BRINGING THE RAIN TO KAPITI PLAIN

A Nandi Tale

BRINGING THE RAIN TO KAPITI PLAIN

retold by Verna Aardema / pictures by Beatriz Vidal

Dial Books for Young Readers / New York

Library of Congress Catalog Card Number: 80-25886
First Pied Piper Printing 1983
Printed in Hong Kong by South China Printing Co.
COBE
10 9 8
A Pied Piper Book is a registered trademark of
Dial Books for Young Readers, a division of Penguin Books USA Inc.
®TM 1,163,686 and ®TM 1,054,312

BRINGING THE RAIN TO KAPITI PLAIN
is published in a hardcover edition by
Dial Books for Young Readers,
375 Hudson Street, New York, New York 10014.
ISBN 0-8037-0904-8

For my librarian,
Bernice Houseward
V. A.

For my parents; for my teacher
B. V.

This is the great
	Kapiti Plain,
All fresh and green
	from the African rains—
A sea of grass for the
	ground birds to nest in,
And patches of shade for
	wild creatures to rest in;
With acacia trees for
	giraffes to browse on,
And grass for the herdsmen
	to pasture their cows on.

But one year the rains
   were so very belated,
That all of the big wild
   creatures migrated.
Then Ki-pat helped to end
   that terrible drought—
And this story tells
   how it all came about!

This is the cloud,
    all heavy with rain,
That shadowed the ground
    on Kapiti Plain.

This is the grass,
    all brown and dead,
That needed the rain
    from the cloud overhead—
The big, black cloud,
    all heavy with rain,
That shadowed the ground
    on Kapiti Plain.

These are the cows,
    all hungry and dry,
Who mooed for the rain
    to fall from the sky;
To green-up the grass,
    all brown and dead,
That needed the rain
    from the cloud overhead—
The big, black cloud,
    all heavy with rain,
That shadowed the ground
    on Kapiti Plain.

This is Ki-pat,
    who watched his herd
As he stood on one leg,
    like the big stork bird;
Ki-pat, whose cows
    were so hungry and dry,
They mooed for the rain
    to fall from the sky;
To green-up the grass,
    all brown and dead,
That needed the rain
    from the cloud overhead—
The big, black cloud,
    all heavy with rain,
That shadowed the ground
    on Kapiti Plain.

This is the eagle
  who dropped a feather,
A feather that helped
  to change the weather.
It fell near Ki-pat,
  who watched his herd
As he stood on one leg,
  like the big stork bird;
Ki-pat, whose cows
  were so hungry and dry,
They mooed for the rain
  to fall from the sky;
To green-up the grass,
  all brown and dead,
That needed the rain
  from the cloud overhead—
The big, black cloud,
  all heavy with rain,
That shadowed the ground
  on Kapiti Plain.

This is the arrow
    Ki-pat put together,
With a slender stick
    and an eagle feather;
From the eagle who happened
    to drop a feather,
A feather that helped
    to change the weather.

It fell near Ki-pat,
    who watched his herd
As he stood on one leg,
    like the big stork bird;
Ki-pat, whose cows
    were so hungry and dry,
They mooed for the rain
    to fall from the sky;
To green-up the grass,
    all brown and dead,
That needed the rain
    from the cloud overhead—
The big, black cloud,
    all heavy with rain,
That shadowed the ground
    on Kapiti Plain.

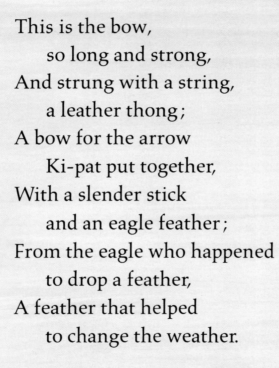

This is the bow,
    so long and strong,
And strung with a string,
    a leather thong;
A bow for the arrow
    Ki-pat put together,
With a slender stick
    and an eagle feather;
From the eagle who happened
    to drop a feather,
A feather that helped
    to change the weather.

It fell near Ki-pat,
    who watched his herd
As he stood on one leg,
    like the big stork bird;
Ki-pat, whose cows
    were so hungry and dry,
They mooed for the rain
    to fall from the sky;
To green-up the grass,
    all brown and dead,
That needed the rain
    from the cloud overhead—
The big, black cloud,
    all heavy with rain,
That shadowed the ground
    on Kapiti Plain.

This was the shot
    that pierced the cloud
And loosed the rain
    with thunder LOUD!
A shot from the bow,
    so long and strong,
And strung with a string,
    a leather thong;
A bow for the arrow
    Ki-pat put together,
With a slender stick
    and an eagle feather;
From the eagle who happened
    to drop a feather,
A feather that helped
    to change the weather.

It fell near Ki-pat,
   who watched his herd
As he stood on one leg,
   like the big stork bird;
Ki-pat, whose cows
   were so hungry and dry,
They mooed for the rain
   to fall from the sky;
To green-up the grass,
   all brown and dead,
That needed the rain
   from the cloud overhead—
The big, black cloud,
   all heavy with rain,
That shadowed the ground
   on Kapiti Plain.

So the grass grew green,
and the cattle fat!
And Ki-pat got a wife
and a little Ki-pat—

Who tends the cows now,
    and shoots down the rain,
When black clouds shadow
    Kapiti Plain.

The Tusk Fairy

For Liberty

The Tusk Fairy

Nicola Smee

Troll Medallion

Lizzie's favorite toy was her knitted Elephant.

Grandma had given him to Lizzie on the
day she was born, so they were exactly
the same age.

They had been through a lot together. . .

and over the years Elephant began to
look the worse for wear.

When Elephant's trunk started to unravel,
Lizzie bandaged it with some ribbon.

When his feet started to wear out and
stuffing poked through his knees,

Lizzie put her doll's socks on Elephant to
keep everything in.

Then, when the wool on Elephant's
back got so thin you could see his
insides, Lizzie removed Teddy's pants.

She put them on Elephant to keep him together.

Then one day a TERRIBLE thing happened!

Lizzie was giving her toys a ride when a thread from Elephant's ear got caught on a thorn.

By the time she noticed, all that was left
of Elephant was two tusks!

Lizzie followed the trail back, picking
up the pants, the socks, bits of stuffing,
the ribbon, and the unraveled wool.

Then she sat down and cried and cried
and cried.
Grandma ran out to see what had happened.

"Why don't you put the tusks under your pillow for the Tooth Fairy?" she said.

So that night, Lizzie put the tusks under her pillow and tried to sleep, while Grandma hunted for some gray wool.

Lizzie fell into a deep dreamy sleep, so she didn't hear Grandma's knitting needles clicking through the night.

The next morning, Grandma was
awakened by Lizzie's cries of delight.
"THE TUSK FAIRY'S BEEN HERE!
THE TUSK FAIRY'S BEEN HERE!"

Grandma was tired but also very happy.
She had been worried when she found
she had run out of gray wool – but it
didn't seem to bother Lizzie.

And fond as they had been of Old
Elephant, the toys were pleased to see
New Elephant, because it meant they got
their clothes back.

For the time being, anyway!

Library of Congress Cataloging-in-Publication Data

Smee, Nicola.
The Tusk Fairy / Nicola Smee.
p.   cm.
Summary: When Lizzie's well-worn knitted elephant unravels
to nothing, leaving only the tusks, Grandma suggests leaving
the remains for the Tooth Fairy to see what will happen.
ISBN 0-8167-3311-2 (lib.)   ISBN 0-8167-3312-0 (pbk.)
[1. Toys–Fiction. 2. Elephants–Fiction. 3. Grandmothers–Fiction.
4. Tooth Fairy–Fiction.] 1. Title.
PZ7.S6396Tu   1994
[E]–dc20   93-28444

Text and illustration copyright © 1994 by Nicola Smee.

Published by Troll Associates, Inc.

First published by ORCHARD BOOKS, 96 Leonard Street,
London EC2A 4RH.

First published in the United States by BridgeWater Books.

Printed in the United States of America.

10 9 8 7 6 3 4 3 2 1